A WOODLAND MYSTERY™

The Secret of the Monster Book

A WOODLAND MYSTERY
By Irene Schultz

The Wright Group®

To Elizabeth Peters and Barbara and Lary Lee, friends of my own Woodland family

The Secret of the Monster Book
©1996 Wright Group Publishing, Inc.
©1996 Story by Irene Schultz
Cover and illustrations by Taylor Bruce
Map illustration by Alicia Kramer

Woodland Mysteries™
© Wright Group Publishing, Inc.

The Woodland Mysteries were created by the
Wright Group development team.

The Wright Group
19201 120th Avenue NE
Bothell, WA 98011

Printed in the United States of America

10 9 8 7 6 5 4 3

ISBN: 0-7802-7235-8

What family solves mysteries...has adventures all over the world...and loves oatmeal cookies?

It's the Woodlanders!

Sammy Westburg (10 years old)
His sister Kathy Westburg (13)
His brother Bill Westburg (14)
His best friend Dave Briggs (16)
His best grown-up friend Mrs. Tandy
And Mop, their little dog!

The children all lost their parents, but with Mrs. Tandy have made their own family.

Why are they called the Woodlanders? Because they live in a big house in the Bluff Lake woods. On Woodland Street!

Together they find fun, mystery, and adventure. What are they up to now?

Read on!

Meet the Woodlanders!

Sammy Westburg
Sammy is a ten-year-old wonder! He's big for his fifth-grade class, and big-mouthed, too. He has wild hair and makes awful spider faces. Even so, you can't help liking him.

Bill Westburg
Bill, fourteen, is friendly and strong, and only one inch taller than his brother Sammy. He loves Sammy, but pokes him to make him be quiet! He's in junior high.

Kathy Westburg
Kathy, thirteen, is small, shy, and smart. She wants to be a doctor some day! She loves to be with Dave, and her brothers kid her about it. She's in junior high, too.

Dave Briggs

Dave, sixteen, is tall and blond. He can't walk, so he uses a wheelchair and drives a special car. He likes coaching high-school sports, solving mysteries, and reading. And Kathy!

Mrs. Tandy

Sometimes the kids call her Mrs. T. She's Becky Tandy, their tall, thin, caring friend. She's always ready for a new adventure, and for making cookies!

Mop

Mop is the family's little tan dog. Sometimes they have to leave him behind with friends. But he'd much rather be running after Sammy.

Table of Contents

Chapter 1:
The Book Appears

Ten-year-old Sammy Westburg held a small book up in the air.

He said, "Hey, what's this? How did THIS get in my bag?"

The four other Woodlanders crowded around him. They were in a hotel room in Japan.

Sammy's brother Bill, fourteen, reached for the book. He said, "Feel how soft it is ... and how it's all hand-stitched along the back edge."

Sammy said, "Who cares about the hand-stitching! Look at the pictures! These are great monsters!"

His thirteen-year-old sister Kathy bent over to see the book. She said, "The writing in it is beautiful. Do you know what kind of book it is, Dave?"

Dave Briggs, sixteen, rolled toward her in his wheelchair. He said, "Well, it's Japanese. And it's printed on soft rice paper.

"You have to read it backward from our books. See, the title of the book is printed on the back cover."

Kathy turned a few pages. She said, "Wow. These monster faces are creepy!"

Mrs. Tandy pointed at one. "I'll say! Look at that dragon. There's fire shooting from its tongue!"

Sammy pointed at a monster with fangs ... and bulging eyes.

He said, "This mad one is YOU, Bill. You're mad because I'm nearly as big as you, and twice as nice."

Then Sammy stuck his tongue out at his brother. He said, "I bet YOU put this book in my bag. You did it just to make me think I'm going crazy!"

Kathy said, "Wait. I've seen this book before. I think I might know how it got into your bag, Sammy. But ... I could be wrong."

Bill said, "Come on, Kathy. How?"

Kathy went on. "Well, just as we were standing up to wheel Dave off the plane at Tokyo ... " She said it like this: TOE-key-oh.

"You know, when almost everyone else had gotten off?

"Well, a tall man was standing next to me. He got off right after we did.

"Don't you remember him, Mrs. T.? The man who kept talking to you at the beginning of the trip?"

Mrs. Tandy said, "Oh, yes, I remember

4

him. He told me he lives in Tokyo.

"He asked me who we were.

"And where we were going.

"And how long we'd be in Japan.

"And where we were going after Japan.

"He seemed very friendly.

"I told him we would be in Japan for a week, then we would be at the King Hotel in Hong Kong."

Kathy said, "Well, when we landed back in Tokyo, he asked me if I'd carry something off the plane for him.

"He said he had a present for his new grand child. He didn't want to ruin it, stuffing it into his bag.

"But I told him I couldn't. The airport folder said not to."

Sammy said, "Not to what? Deliver presents to little kids?"

Kathy laughed. "No, Sammy. Not to bring anything through customs check for anyone else."

Dave said, "Good move, Kathy. They're afraid of smugglers."

Kathy said, "Anyway, maybe he just sneaked the book into Sammy's bag."

Sammy laughed and said, "That's a drippy idea! I had my bag with me the whole time."

Bill said, "Kathy, ignore this laughing hyena. When do you think it could've happened?"

Kathy said, "I bet that man slipped it

into the pocket of Sammy's bag when we were getting Dave off the plane!

"I put the bags down so I could help you. He could have done it then."

Sammy said, "But then he would have asked for it back when we left customs ... unless he forgot it."

Bill said, "When you think about it, isn't it sort of a funny present for a baby? A soft book would be easy to ruin. A little kid could even eat it."

Mrs. Tandy nodded. "And a book of monsters isn't exactly what you'd give a young child."

Kathy said, "And it's weird that he'd slip it into someone else's bag."

Dave said, "But that isn't the weirdest thing of all."

Sammy jumped up and said, "Oh, yeah, then what is?"

Dave said, "This is. We passed about

a thousand books just like this one in the book stands at the Tokyo airport. Piles of them.

"Then I saw more after the flight to Osaka."

Sammy shouted, "Oh-SOCK-uh!" and socked Bill on the arm.

Dave went on. "And I saw more after the bus trip here. This book is made in Japan. He could have bought one any-where in this country.

"Why would he buy a Japanese book in the United States ... and carry it back to Japan ... as a present for a baby who would probably eat it ... and would be scared by the monster pictures ... and couldn't even read it?

"And why would he put it in Sammy's bag?"

Chapter 2:
Someone's Been Here

Bill said, "Well, just put the book in the dresser, Sammy. I guess it's your book now.

"Let's un-pack and head out. I want

to get a look at Kyoto, now that we are here." He said it like this: Key-OH-toe.

Mrs. Tandy and Kathy went through the doorway to their room.

Sammy un-packed the fastest.

He turned his bag upside-down ... and mashed his clothes into the dresser drawers.

Then he bragged, "Hah, slowpokes, I'm done. I beat you all!"

He got a glass of water to drink and sat down with the monster book.

Bill said, "Watch out, Sammy. Don't spill the water on your book."

Sammy said, "You're always trying to boss me, Bill. I won't spill it.

"Oops! Well, I did drip a little onto a couple of words. Hey, look! The print on one of the words ran a little. That's weird."

Bill said, "You're just lucky they didn't ALL run. Here, take this tissue and blot up the water. Let's get going."

They met Mrs. Tandy and Kathy in the hall.

On the way out, Dave said, "What should we see first? A school? A palace? A Japanese garden?"

Sammy said, "How do you know about all that stuff, Dave?"

Dave said, "From a library book. I even made a copy of a map that was in it."

Sammy rubbed his belly and said, "Well, I hope it had the name of a place to have BREAKFAST. That's what I want to see first. I'm hungry enough to eat a worm."

Mrs. Tandy smiled. "I can help find breakfast. I heard about a wonderful old inn. It's supposed to have great food. I even have the address."

Dave said, "Let's go find it!"

They walked for blocks and blocks, past wooden houses and shops.

Kathy said, "It's so clean! Even if some of it's old, it looks beautiful."

Dave nodded. "I read that people here sweep their sidewalks every day."

Mrs. Tandy was looking all around. She said, "Well, I guess someone swept the inn away! We should be there by now, but where is it?"

A Japanese man was walking along

behind them. He wore a neat business suit. He carried a briefcase.

Mrs. Tandy smiled at him and said, "I hate to bother you, but could you help us? Do you understand English?"

He nodded yes. She showed him the name of the inn.

Smiling, but silent, the man led them to a plain wooden door.

Mrs. Tandy said, "Thank you."

The man only smiled and gave a little bow.

13

So Mrs. Tandy bowed back.

The man bowed to each of the Woodlanders in turn. They bowed back.

He bowed once more to them all. They all bowed again. Finally he walked away.

Bill said, "Have we seen him before?"

Sammy said, "Don't be a drip. We don't know anyone in Japan."

Bill said, "I know I've seen his face somewhere ... the way his eyebrows slant down at the sides ... and that scar on his chin."

Sammy shook his head and said, "I hate to tell you this, Bill. You're so hungry you've gone crazy. Let's go inside and eat."

The woman who owned the inn said, "You look tired. Come in and rest."

She took them to a big room. Light flowed in through its rice-paper walls.

A shiny black table, hardly higher than a footstool, stood in the middle.

The floor was covered with thick, soft, woven straw mats.

The inn owner placed five wooden backrests around the table.

Sammy said, "I love this!"

Dave lowered himself from his wheelchair to the floor. He leaned against a backrest. The others followed him down.

A woman in a silk robe brought them breakfast.

Each kind of food was in a different bowl.

First came an orange-brown soup with seaweed on top.

Sammy said, "Ick! Slime!" But when he tasted it, he loved it.

Then they ate tiny yellow vegetables, tied with thin ribbons of green onion.

They ate sharp-tasting yellow pickles

with threads of red beets.

They ate small chunks of raw fish.

Last they had rice crackers with a sweet spread on top.

Kathy said, "It's the prettiest breakfast I ever ate."

They thanked the inn owner and went back to the hotel to rest.

Sammy went to his dresser to get his monster book.

A minute later they heard him yell, "Someone's been in our room! Someone looked at my book while we were gone!"

Chapter 3:
Mrs. Tandy's Old Friend

Mrs. Tandy said, "What makes you think that, Sammy?"

Sammy pointed at the book.

He said, "Look here! I stuck the hotel

shoehorn into the book to keep it open. I wanted the page to dry out. You know, where I spilled a drop of water."

Dave said, "The shoehorn IS stuck into it, Sammy."

Sammy shook his head and said, "But I stuck the FRONT end in. And look, now it's stuck in handle-first."

Mrs. Tandy said, "Maybe you're just forgetting, honey. We were in a hurry to get out this morning."

Sammy said, "I'm NOT forgetting! I put the front end in because it would hold the book open wider ... so it would dry faster.

"Besides, look here. It's not even at the right page. The page where I stuck it in had that runny word on it."

Bill said, "I bet I know what happened. They probably came in to clean the room.

"They moved the book and the shoe-horn fell out ... so they stuck it back in."

Kathy said, "That would explain it, Sammy."

Mrs. Tandy said, "So let's grab an hour of sleep. Then we can go sight-seeing again."

By noon they were ready to look around town again.

They left their hotel room.

Bill stopped to talk to the woman behind the front desk. She was from the United States. Her name was Wendy.

Sammy poked Bill and whispered, "I bet you don't even have a question. You're just talking to her because she's so pretty."

Finally Sammy said, "I'm tired of waiting for you. I'm going back up to get my monster book. I'll be right down."

Ten minutes later they were still waiting for Sammy.

19

Bill said, "What's taking him so long? I'm going up after him."

Just then Sammy came running out of the elevator.

His face was red.

His hair was sticking up all over.

Mrs. Tandy said, "Honey, what's wrong?"

Sammy gasped and said, "My book! My monster book! Someone stole it off the dresser!"

Bill said, "Oh, come on, Sammy. Why would anyone steal your book? I'll go up with you and help you find it."

Dave said, "Maybe one of us looked at it, and just forgot to put it back where you left it."

Sammy said, "No, it's gone. I searched both rooms."

Then he looked a little guilty. He said, "I even searched through everyone's drawers ... but not yours, Mrs. Tandy, don't worry.

"And I saw a picture of Kathy in your drawer, Dave."

Kathy turned red.

Dave turned redder.

Sammy went on. "But I couldn't find my book anywhere."

Mrs. Tandy said, "Well, come to think of it, I was looking at it before you woke up. I could have left it in my drawer."

Sammy felt silly. He said, "Oh, well, then ... I guess we don't have to go back up. That's where it is, I guess. So let's take our walk."

The Woodlanders walked through the zoo.

They walked past garden ponds and watched huge gold and black fish swimming through the water. They walked past a candy store ... and through a museum.

Finally Sammy said, "I give up. I'm all walked out. I think I'm dead. My feet don't want to see one more inch of Kyoto."

So they all dragged back to the hotel.

They found Wendy waiting for them.

She had a worried look on her face.

She said, "One of our cleaning crew did something she shouldn't have. She thought it would be all right, since she stayed right with him.

"She let a man into your rooms ... just a few minutes before you came back. He said he was an old high-school friend of yours, Mrs. Tandy.

"And he had found something of yours. He put it on one of the dressers.

"I hope it's all right."

They rushed to their rooms.

Sammy dashed over to his dresser.

There was the monster book, safe and sound.

Sticking out of it was an envelope. Inside the envelope was a note:

Dear Becky Tandy,

It has been such a long time since high school. I am so glad you are in town at last. I have planned a dinner for us near the Saga train stop, 45 minutes away. You will find five round-trip tickets in this envelope. Meet me at the Saga River Inn at 7:00 p.m. And bring this charming book. I will be glad to tell you all about it.

Sincerely, your old school friend,

Yoshi Mori

P.S. Please come!

Kathy said, "How exciting! I didn't know you had an old friend here, Mrs. Tandy!"

Dave said, "Great! We can see another Japanese town!"

Bill added, "And I bet the dinner will be WONDERFUL!"

And Sammy sang out, "Mrs. Tandy has a boyfriend ... Mrs. Tandy has a boyfriend."

But Mrs. Tandy said, "There's just one problem, Sammy. You know this good old school friend of mine? Yoshi Mori?

"Well, I've never heard of him in my whole life."

Chapter 4:
Should We Go?

Dave said, "Are you SURE?"

Sammy said, "Don't you remember a name a little LIKE Yoshi Mori?"

Mrs. Tandy shook her head. "Unless

I'm losing my memory, I never knew a Yoshi Mori ... or any other Mori."

Bill said, "Think hard, Mrs. T. Maybe there was a special student at your high school. One from Japan?

"One who changed places with a student from the United States?"

Mrs. Tandy said, "Honey, I hate to disappoint you ... but I just can't think of a soul with that name. Not even close."

Sammy said, "ROTTEN RATS! I was already thinking how much fun it would be to ride on a Japanese train."

Kathy said, "And now we have to throw out five train tickets.

"Or do you think we can return them?

"And how would we give the money back to this Yoshi Mori person?"

Dave said, "Just a minute here! Not so fast. Maybe we should go to Saga anyway.

"I'm wondering how this person could have made a mistake like this.

"So let's say for a minute he DIDN'T make a mistake.

"Let's say he never DID know Mrs. Tandy.

"Let's say for some reason he wants to talk to her. Or to all of us. Let's say it's important, but he wants to do it in secret."

29

Bill said, "If that's true, I guess he might pretend he knew her ... in case he thought he was being watched."

Sammy clapped his hands. "Boy oh boy! This sounds better and better! It sounds like a spy mystery!

"But ... wait a minute.

"A spy wouldn't be interested in a monster book, would he?"

Mrs. Tandy said, "Well, I'm beginning to get the feeling anything is possible!

"Anyway, we have an hour or so before we have to take the train ... that is, if we want to go.

"Let's think about it for a while."

Sammy sat down with his book.

He said, "I'm sure glad to have my book back. If that guy found it ... one of you must have carried it out into the hall and dropped it. So WHO WAS IT?"

He patted the book as if it were a dog.

He said, "I'm glad that the man on the plane gave this to me, even by mistake.

"I'm going to look at every single picture in it.

"Maybe I'll try drawing some monsters, too ... like the ones in the book.

"I'll use the same wild colors.

"I bet I can draw really scary monsters. I'll just get Bill to pose."

Bill smiled and said, "You don't need me to pose. You could just make your poison-spider face, look in the mirror, and draw that."

Sammy sat down and began to turn page after page in the book.

He looked at it from cover to cover.

Then Bill saw him start all over again.

This time Sammy searched over every page carefully. He looked at every single line.

Bill said, "What's wrong, Sammy? Trying to learn Japanese?"

Sammy said, "HERE'S what's wrong! You know that runny word? The one that I messed up when I dropped water on it?

"Well, I can't find that page.

"I looked and looked.

"I know the water dried up, but the word that ran should still look runny.

"But I can't find it anywhere!"

Bill pulled up a chair next to Sammy.

He said, "Here, let me look."

He couldn't find the runny word, either.

He called Dave over.

Mrs. Tandy and Kathy came in from their room.

The whole group went through the book three times.

They couldn't find the runny word.

Finally Sammy said, "You know what? The runny word isn't here. And you know what else? This isn't my book."

Bill said, "I think Sammy's right. Something weird is going on."

Dave said, "I think we should use those tickets and find out. Let's go to Saga."

Chapter 5:
Who Is Mr. Mori?

At 6:45 they got off the train at Saga.

Sammy said, "Boy, that train was clean! I loved riding in it.

"It was so nice, it made me feel

important. So now I'm your leader! Follow me!"

He led them down to the river.

Then he said, "Stop! We aren't going into the inn yet!"

He pointed toward the river. "I want to go see what that man catches. I'm not moving until he gets a fish."

Sammy set his feet apart like a stubborn mule.

The man was fishing in the middle of a river as wide as a cornfield.

Suddenly the man jerked his long, bamboo fishing pole upward.

But the end of it stayed bent down toward the water.

It wiggled and jiggled and bounced up and down.

Sammy shouted, "He's got one! I bet it's a huge one!"

He cupped his hands toward the man

and shouted, "Don't let it break your line! Play it in the water till it's good and tired!"

Just then the man pulled the fish up. It hung in the air.

Bill laughed, "There's your huge one, Sammy."

Sammy said, "Hey! It's tiny! What a rip-off!"

He pinched Bill on the arm and said, "You shouldn't have wasted our time ... standing here watching that guy."

Bill groaned, "You know, Sammy, you're a real pest."

He looked mad ... but only for a minute.

Sammy headed toward the inn.

The others followed him inside.

A woman in a beautiful red-and-white silk robe bowed to them.

They all bowed back.

37

Sammy whispered to Bill, "Here we go, bowing again. But I'm getting used to it. In fact, I sort of like it."

Dave said to the woman, "This is Mrs. Tandy. These are the three Westburgs. And I'm Dave Briggs.

"We are supposed to meet a man here ... Mr. Yoshi Mori?"

The woman smiled. "Oh, yes. Follow me, please. Mr. Mori is here. But can

you get up the steps with your wheelchair, Mr. Briggs?"

Sammy answered, "Sure he can!" and
grabbed hold of the back of Dave's
wheelchair.

Quickly they carried Dave to the
second floor, into a dining room.

Like the breakfast room that morning,
the room had rice-paper walls.

Part of one wall was open, from the
floor to the roof. Through the branches
of a tree they could look out at the river.

On the floor, behind a low table, sat
a Japanese man. His hands rested in his
lap. He was dressed in a blue silk
robe ... with gold and silver dragons all
over it.

He looked like a painting of an important Japanese leader.

The next moment the man got up
and walked toward them.

The long sleeves of his robe shone with gold and silver threads.

He bowed and said, "I am Yoshi Mori. Welcome! I'm so glad you came."

The others bowed, but not Sammy. He walked right up to Mr. Mori.

He stuck his head forward like a duck.

He looked right into the man's face.

He said, "Hey, what IS this?

"I know you. We talked to you today. You're the guy who showed us how to get to breakfast. My brother thought he knew you.

"You acted like you hardly spoke English. Were you following us or what?"

Yoshi Mori smiled and pointed toward the low dining table.

He said, "Sit down, please. Let's talk while we eat."

They sat down on the floor and began their dinner.

40

Mr. Mori said, "I do speak English, but I have forgotten much. I went to college in the United States.

"And of course I speak Japanese. And French, and some German. And yes, I was following you."

Kathy said, "But why would you follow US?"

Mr. Mori said, "I had to find out if you were up to something crooked. Now I feel sure you are all right."

Dave said, "Just a minute. How do you know we AREN'T crooks? You've only seen us once before, when you followed us ... or am I wrong?"

Mr. Mori smiled. "I must confess, I have seen more of you than that. In fact, I was on your plane from the United States."

Bill said, "I KNEW I had seen you before!"

Mr. Mori said, "I watched our suspect, a Mr. Bo Lee, for the entire trip. I saw him speak with Mrs. Tandy."

Mrs. Tandy said, "Please, call me Becky."

Mr. Mori smiled and went on. "And I saw him put a book into Sammy's bag as you were getting off the plane.

"That's why I thought you might be a part of his smuggling ring ... or at least the charming Becky Tandy might be."

Mrs. Tandy said, "ME? A SMUGGLER?"

Sammy giggled. "Mrs. T.? She can't even keep a secret when she bakes a pie for a surprise! She always has a smear of flour on her chin. Some smuggler!"

Mr. Mori said, "Just the same, I called the police chief of your town, a Chief John Hemster."

Bill said, "But wait a minute! How could you have seen the man dump the book on Sammy? He was the last one off the plane. No one was behind him!"

Dave said, "No one but the flight attendant."

Bill said, "THE FLIGHT ATTENDANT! You were the flight attendant! You served us our meals. THAT'S where I saw you!"

Kathy said shyly, "But ... you must

43

have been faking it. That's not your real job, is it?"

Mr. Mori held out his wallet to show them a card.

It read:

Yoshi Mori

Chief Detective
Interpol
Japan

Chapter 6:
Inside the Monster Book

Dave looked at the wallet.

He passed it around to the others.

He said, "Well, Mr. Mori, it looks like what you say is true. You're a detective with the world-wide police force!"

Mr. Mori nodded. He said, "Now finish your dinner. We will talk more when you're done."

Dish after dish, they emptied the beautiful bowls of food.

Sammy wiped his mouth with one of the warm, damp cloths the woman brought them.

Then he scrubbed away with it at some spots on his shirt front.

Finally he grinned. "I'm not so good at eating with chopsticks.

"Oh, well. At least I'll have this shirt to help me remember this meal. I have a little sample of every food we ate, right here on my stomach.

"It was the strangest food I ever had, and the prettiest."

Mr. Mori smiled and bowed slightly toward Sammy.

Sammy tried to bow, but instead he BURPED!

Bill was so embarrassed, he closed his eyes. He couldn't bear to look at Mr. Mori. Kathy looked ready to faint.

But Sammy just said, "Sorry, Mr. Mori. I can't bow back. My stomach's so full of great food, it won't bend."

Mr. Mori laughed and bowed again.

He said, "Your words are thanks enough. I'm glad you liked it."

Bill said, "Mr. Mori, now tell us why you asked us here.

"Mrs. Tandy has the monster book right here in her purse. Maybe you'll tell us about it, too."

Mrs. Tandy took out the book.

At the same moment Mr. Mori pulled a book out of the sleeve of his robe.

Sammy said, "Your book is just like my book ... but my book isn't really my book because some crook—"

Mr. Mori broke in. "Sammy, THIS book is your book. I took yours from your room this afternoon. I left that copy in its place.

"Your book is a treasure that Interpol had to copy."

Bill said, "So that explains everything! You had Sammy's book!"

Sammy wrinkled his nose. He looked mad. He said, "Why did you play a trick on me?"

Mr. Mori said, "I'm sorry. It was important that I have a chance to examine this book.

"We know that Bo Lee, our suspect, needs this book very badly.

"Today I discovered exactly why it is worth so much to him ... why he carried it all over the U.S. with him ...

"Also why he wanted you to carry it through customs ... why he paid to get into your room this morning ... and why he had to make sure the book was safely there."

Sammy said, "Well, why?"

Mr. Mori went on. "You see, Bo Lee traveled all over your country. He went to eleven U.S. cities.

"He found crooks who would pay big money for stolen diamonds.

"Now, here's why this book is so important to him. He has written their

49

names and addresses in this book. It is his only written record.

"We found he added lines on eleven different pages.

"He made his writing match the words in the book EXACTLY."

Kathy said, "So Bo Lee is Japanese, too?"

Mr. Mori said, "No. He's Chinese. Based out of Hong Kong."

Sammy had been thinking. He gasped, "So Bo Lee wrote stuff in the monster book. And THAT'S why the ink ran on that page!"

Then Sammy explained, "See, I sort of spilled just a teeny drop of water on the book."

Mr. Mori nodded.

He said, "I saw that. Bo Lee figured the book could go through customs ... and the hand-written lines wouldn't be noticed.

"But he wasn't sure. Lee has been questioned by customs and Interpol before.

"He couldn't chance being caught with this book on him.

"So he stuck the book into your bag. The customs people wouldn't check your bags as carefully as his. You don't really look like crooks."

Mrs. Tandy smiled. "Why, thank you!"

Mr. Mori smiled back. "Anyway, Bo Lee didn't know it, but Interpol trailed him all the way.

"We know how he works. We've been watching him. We think he's been cheating customs for two years. But we didn't know how.

"We knew you were stuck with the book. But I told customs to let it go right through with you.

"I don't want Lee to know we are watching him this trip."

Sammy said, "Then HE'S the one who moved my shoehorn! He was checking everything out!"

Kathy said, "But what about when Sammy couldn't find his book this afternoon?"

Mr. Mori said, "I saw our suspect go to the lobby.

"He had already checked to make sure

the book was safe. So I took it to get a good look at it.

"But then I saw you come back for it, Sammy.

"You couldn't find it and finally left. But what if you decided to look for it again, and I was still there? Or what if Lee took a quick look in?

"So I rushed to the gift shop in the lobby. I bought another copy. I put the new copy on your dresser with my note.

"By then I had decided to ask you to help Interpol."

Dave said, "But Mr. Mori! The problem is worse than ever!

"Chances are, Mr. Lee checked our room for the book when we came here. He must have discovered we took it with us.

"He wouldn't want to let us out of his sight ... even for a minute ... until the book's back in his hands. This book is worth millions of dollars to him.

"Maybe he's even followed us here!"

Sammy slid away from his backrest. He rolled over on his stomach.

Like a scared beetle, he crawled quickly across the floor. He stopped at the opening in the wall.

He sneaked a look below.

He cried, "Good grief! I think that's Mr. Lee standing right down there. And he's watching the door of this inn!"

Chapter 7:
Spying on the Spy

Mr. Mori said, "Never fear, Wonder Yoshi is here!"

The Woodlanders looked at him, surprised.

He said, "Sorry. I heard something like that on TV in your country, years ago.

"But it's true. I'm always there when trouble comes ... or at the very least I'll have another Interpol agent on the spot."

Dave said, "So you've been spying on the spy who's watching us?"

Mr. Mori said, "Yes. He will be watching you every minute you carry his book with you.

"He will follow you in Japan, and in Hong Kong, until he takes back his book. And we will be following him."

Bill said, "So you KNEW he'd be right outside here!"

Mr. Mori nodded. "We wanted him to come to Saga. We wanted to SEE him here, to make sure we were right about him.

"We figured if we could make him nervous, he would become careless about keeping hidden.

"So we made it impossible for him to tell where the book was."

Sammy crawled back from the opening and sat up to listen.

Mr. Mori went on. "Today, the instant you left your rooms, one of my team moved in.

"He sprayed your room.

"Then he put a sign across the door that said DO NOT ENTER. POISON INSECT SPRAY. UN-SAFE UNTIL 11 P.M.

"Lee wouldn't dare open that door. So he couldn't check your room."

Sammy made some choking sounds.

"That's disGUSTing! What are you trying to do? Kill us off like bugs?"

Mr. Mori laughed. "Don't worry. The smell will have worn off by the time you get there. It will be safe for you."

Sammy said, "Mr. Mori, I've got to hand it to you. You really know how to pester a person! In fact, you're almost as good as me ... and I'm the champ!"

Mr. Mori laughed again and said, "Thank you. That's high praise indeed."

Sammy said, "But I've got a question. How come you don't arrest him right now? I could even jump on him from up here.

"Then you could run out the front door and grab him.

"I saw a cowboy jump from the second story in a movie once. He landed right on the bad guy."

Sammy stopped for a minute. "On second thought, if I jumped on him, there might not be enough left of him to arrest. We'd have to scrape him up with a pancake turner."

Mr. Mori smiled and said, "We don't want to do anything to him now. Not even turn him into a pancake.

"We feel sure that he plans to smuggle diamonds. But we can't arrest him until he actually does it.

"So the help we need from you is to take good care of Lee's book! Here, and when you go to Hong Kong.

"In fact, while I'm thinking about it, let's trade books. We have copied what we need from Lee's book.

"I know he will leave it with you until he's ready to leave Hong Kong himself.

"But he will watch over it, and you, every second.

"That will make our job of keeping track of him easier.

"My team will be watching both him and you."

Kathy said, "But what if we see Mr. Lee and he knows we saw him? And he knows we know he's the man we met on the plane to Japan?"

Mr. Mori said, "Well, then, he would have to pretend to want to be your friend on the rest of the trip.

"He would pretend he didn't even want the book back.

"If he acts friendly, you act friendly."

Mr. Mori looked at his watch. "And now, you have plenty of time to walk back to the train station.

"The train will not come until ten o'clock.

"Lee will have plenty of time to follow you there.

"He will hide out until you get on the train."

Sammy growled, "I hope he gets really bored!"

Mr. Mori smiled. He said, "I think he's too nervous to be bored!

"Would you be good enough to go into your hotel room at eleven thirty, sharp?

"Then, a little later, decide to go out for a midnight snack?

"Leave Lee's book in your room. He will check to see that his book is safe."

Mrs. Tandy said, "Mr. Mori, thank you for this wonderful dinner. I feel like you ARE an old friend!"

Dave added, "It was great, and I know we all would be glad to help Interpol.

"But we have to make a phone call first, to the United States. So we will give you our answer tomorrow."

Sammy said, "Oh, come off it, Dave! Who do we have to phone?"

But Mr. Mori nodded and gave a small smile.

He said, "You are wise beyond your years, Dave. Here is a number where you can reach me. Call me when you are sure."

The Woodlanders got on the 10:00 train to Kyoto.

Sure enough, they saw a man sneaking aboard at the last minute.

Sammy said, "Well, old Lee's safe and sound in the last car."

In an hour they were back at the hotel lobby.

At 11:30 they went straight to their rooms.

They took the insect-spray warning off the door.

As soon as they got inside, Dave picked up the phone.

Sammy said, "I still don't see—"

He and Bill watched Dave dial and wait for the ring.

In a minute they heard him say, "Hello! Chief Hemster? This is Dave Briggs.

"I'm glad to hear your voice, too.

We miss you! I'm calling to check out a man who claims he's an Interpol agent. He said he called you about us.

"His name is Yoshi Mori. Will you call me in the morning about him?"

Then they left the room for their midnight snack.

Chapter 8:
The Wild Goose Chase

It was early the next morning.

Someone knocked on the door.

Sammy groaned and rolled over onto his stomach.

He buried his face in his pillow and pretended to snore.

Bill jumped out of bed and opened the door.

There stood a waiter, with a cart full of covered dishes.

He rolled the cart in fast, stepped inside, and closed the door.

Bill said, "We didn't order breakfast. There must be a mistake."

Sammy lifted his head from the pillow like a sleepy old turtle. He said, "Are you kidding? Breakfast is NEVER a mistake."

The waiter smiled and said, "I'm just following orders from the hotel manager. He had a phone call and a fax for Dave Briggs."

Dave said, "That's me!"

The waiter went on. "Then he gave me orders to deliver the fax in secret."

He looked at Sammy. "Sorry, but this isn't breakfast."

He lifted a silver cover from one of the plates and left.

On the plate lay a fax.

It was from Police Chief Hemster. It had Yoshi Mori's picture on it. It said he was an Interpol agent ... and could be trusted.

Mrs. Tandy and Kathy walked in just as the waiter left.

Kathy said, "Wow! Breakfast?"

Bill said, "Nope. It's a fax from Chief Hemster! It says Yoshi Mori is who he says he is."

Dave called Mr. Mori to tell him they would be glad to help him.

Then Bill went over to Sammy's bed. He said, "All right, turtle. Don't fall asleep again.

"Let's get going. We only have five days left in Kyoto before flying to Hong Kong."

Sammy jumped out of bed. He said, "I was just resting a little so I'd be ready for today.

"Dave and I made a map last night for our walk today. Show it to them, Dave!

"See, first we eat breakfast ... then we walk to this temple ... and walk through its gardens.

"Then we walk to this palace ... and

walk through ITS gardens.

"Next we walk to a place where they have all kinds of shows."

Bill said, "Just a minute! Yesterday you said you couldn't take one more step.

"Today you've planned a walk that would kill an elephant. I don't get it!"

Sammy smiled an innocent smile. He batted his eyelashes.

Mrs. Tandy said, "You look like an angel, but I know you too well. That innocent look means you have something up your sleeve. So what is it?"

Sammy said, "It's a GREAT plan, that's what!

"See, first you put the monster book in your purse, Mrs. T.

"Mr. Lee looks for the book in our room. He sees we have it with us.

"So all day long he follows us. And we take him on a wild goose chase!

"We wear him out for Interpol!"

Now Dave smiled the same innocent smile as Sammy's. He nodded and said, "That's not just a great plan, it's a PERFECT plan!"

So they got dressed, took the book, and started out for the lobby.

Dave said, "Don't leave the lobby too fast. Give him enough time to find out we have the book with us. Wait for him to get on our trail."

They waited for a few minutes. Then they left the hotel lobby.

After walking two blocks, Sammy said, "Wait up. I'll check to make sure he's back there.

"I'll go around this corner and run around the block. I'll be able to see him from behind.

"You guys stop here. Pretend you're reading the map."

In a while Sammy was back.

He giggled, "Saw him!

"He's at the corner, a block behind us.

"He's hiding behind his newspaper. He's pretending to read it.

"He's wearing a gray suit and a white shirt with thin blue stripes. And he's wearing dark sunglasses.

"There really should be a law against bad guys buying newspapers."

Sammy went on. "But there's no law against spying on a spy. So every ten minutes or so, one of us can check on Mr. Lee. After all, we don't want him to lose us."

By the end of the day they had climbed around the palace ... seen shady moss gardens ... and looked at golden temple walls.

They had walked over floors built to squeak when people were coming ... and had seen a tea ceremony ... a dance show ... a puppet act ... and a play.

Every night after that, Dave and Sammy drew up a new walking map for the next day.

And every morning they took the monster book and walked their legs off!

Late the fifth night they packed their suitcases.

They took the bus to the Kyoto airport.

They boarded the plane bound for Hong Kong, just off the coast of China.

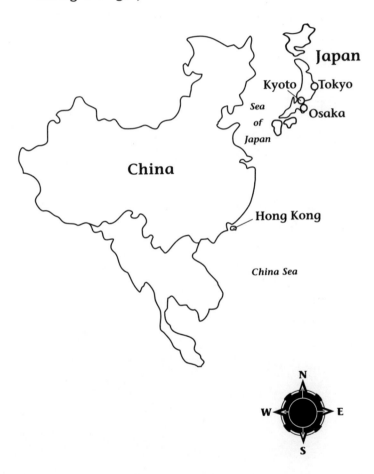

They were tired, VERY tired ... but Mr. Lee was a MESS!

He limped into a limo to get to the airport.

He pulled his coat collar up to hide his face.

He dragged himself aboard their plane. He sneaked to the back and fell into his seat.

He was too far back to hear Sammy whisper, "Boy, I can't wait to take Mr. Lee on the NEXT wild goose chase!

"Hong Kong, here we come!"

Chapter 9:
Wednesday, Bird Street

Kathy looked out the plane window.

She cried out, "Hong Kong at night is so pretty!"

She went on. "It looks like a light

show on a fairy hill. Or a bunch of jewels shining on black velvet cloth!"

Dave groaned. "I'm almost too tired to open my eyes to see it."

Mrs. Tandy, Bill, and Sammy were sleeping.

When the plane touched down, Sammy woke up. He said, "I hope we aren't there yet. I'm too tired to move."

It was 5:00 in the morning when they fell into their hotel beds.

Mrs. Tandy woke up with a start. She looked at her watch. It said 7:00.

Through the door to the boys' room she heard a shout.

"NOW I've got you! You're a DEAD man!"

She jumped up. She threw open the door between the two rooms.

A balled-up pair of socks hit her right on the chin.

Dave called, "Oops. Sorry, Mrs. T.!

"Hope I didn't hurt you. We were just having a sock war."

Mrs. Tandy said, "It's just seven o'clock. We've only had two hours of sleep, but I feel much better.

"My, but it's dark this morning!"

Sammy said, "Morning? It's seven o'clock at night! We slept right through one whole day!"

Mrs. Tandy looked disappointed. "You mean we've lost a day of seeing Hong Kong?"

Bill nodded. "Today's Tuesday already. We fly home next Monday morning. That leaves us only a few days here.

"Let's eat here in the hotel and make plans for the rest of the trip!"

At the King Hotel restaurant they checked the menu.

Sammy said, "Yuck! This is different from the Chinese food place back home in Bluff Lake!

"This menu has some of the worst things I ever saw!"

Dave said, "They're just strange to us. Remember, you thought Japanese food was weird at first, too.

"We should each order something different. Then maybe you'll like at least one thing, Sammy."

Sammy said, "Well, then, I'm going to order something really awful ... something worse than any food YOU guys order.

"Ah, here it is. Soup made from the webs of duck feet."

Bill said, "I've got a better one. It's got shark fin in it."

Kathy pointed at her menu. "Well, here's what I'm ordering. Bird's nest soup."

Dave said, "I'm getting chicken feet!"

Mrs. Tandy closed her menu. "Well, I hate to disappoint you, but I'm ordering a plain steamed fish."

Sammy groaned. "Steamed fish? That doesn't sound too good, either."

While they waited for their food Dave made this list:

79

Things to do in Hong Kong
Wednesday
   1. Bird Street and the Jade Market
   2. Take ferry
   3. Shop at street booths
Thursday
   1. Hong Kong Island
   2 Zoo and flower gardens
   3. Explore
Friday
   1. The old walled city in the mountains
Saturday
   1. Hollywood Road
Sunday
   1. Rest and pack for home

Sammy looked up. "Yuck! The food's coming!"

But those were his last words until the end of the meal. As it turned out, he loved everything ... even the chicken feet.

After all the food was gone, he patted his stomach.

He said, "See? I TOLD you we'd like this food."

At 6:00 the next morning they arrived at Bird Street.

Dave said, "Now, slow down, guys. Don't let Mr. Lee lose us."

Every inch of the short street was crowded with little stands.

An old man walking by held a bird cage. He was showing off his pet.

Sammy said, "Boy, I bet he can find everything here his bird could ever want. Look at those bamboo cages. They're really pretty."

Mrs. Tandy said, "I know! I want one of those!

"And look at those fancy carved sticks

for birds to stand on.   And a million kinds of seeds."

Dave pointed. "Those are cuttlebones, for birds to sharpen their beaks on.

"They're really shells ... from the insides of cuttlefish!"

Sammy said, "You're kidding me! They're from inside those squid things?"

Kathy nodded. "Listen to all these birds. It sounds like a jungle."

Bill said, "Check out those bird toys. And those little blue-and-white cups, for birds to eat out of."

Mrs. Tandy said, "Oh, my! Just look at all the birds. Boxes and cages and crates of lovely birds!"

Bill added, "But look how crowded they are. How can they even stay alive? They're gasping for air."

Then he took a good look at a stand to his right. "Holy hot dogs! This place is crawling with bugs!"

He was pointing at a glass case that was as big as the back seat of a car. It was CRAWLING with big pale green insects.

They looked like grasshoppers.

They were moving all over the floor and sides of the case, even over each other.

Then Mrs. Tandy pointed to some bags packed with the insects. She said, "Why, birds must eat them for a treat, like we eat french fries!"

Sammy said, "Yuck! Let's go. I decided I don't like it here after all. I just thought, what if I were one of the birds in the cage?

"No matter how nice your owner was, you'd still be a prisoner."

He turned back and said, "Wait! Hold everything! I see Mr. Lee hiding behind a pile of cages. I have an idea. Wait for me here."

Sammy walked over to an insect stand.

He laid down some Hong Kong money on the counter.

He picked up a bag of insects.

Then he disappeared into the crowd.

Chapter 10:
Fire Alarm!

Mrs. Tandy looked very worried.

She said, "My stars! Where did Sammy go? How will we find him in this crowd?"

Bill said, "Don't worry. Sammy will come back."

He sounded calm, but he was plenty worried, too.

Then, before he could start to look for him, Sammy was back. And he was GRINNING.

All he said was, "I'll tell you where I was later. Back to our wild goose chase. Head for the Jade Market. Step on it, Dave. Fast!"

Half the time they had to trot to keep up with Dave. They looked like a fast parade.

The weather was hot and damp, and the Woodlanders were starting to sweat.

Mrs. Tandy was carrying a cage she had bought on Bird Street.

She gasped, "Oh, my! Everyone's staring at us. Can't blame them, though.

"I'm about a foot and a half taller

than most of the people around here.

"And I'm leaping along carrying a bird cage.

"I must look like a crazy kangaroo!"

At last, panting like dogs, they came to an open square.

People selling jade sat at hundreds of little tables.

Mrs. Tandy said, "Look. Jade everywhere. And the colors ... browns, greens, whites, even violets.

"And look at all those other beautiful stones."

Sammy groaned, "I'm so tired from running, I can't even look."

Bill said, "Well, I see something that's going to make you feel better. Across the square, guys!

"I see Mr. Lee, and HE'S A MESS! Don't all turn to look at once."

One by one, they sneaked a peek.

There stood Mr. Lee, body all drooping, sweating like a wrestler.

He was carrying his coat jacket.

Sweat made his shirt dark around his neck and arms.

He was wiggling like a dog with fleas.

He kept brushing himself off all over ... first his hair ... then his shoulders ... his back ... his arms ... then his hair again.

Then he took hold of his belt and shook his pants.

Then he shook his pant legs, one at a time.

Then he stamped his feet.

Bill said, "My gosh, he looks like he has the heebie-jeebies!"

Mrs. Tandy smiled. "I'd say he looks like he has ants in his pants!"

Sammy gave a little fake laugh. "Yek, yek, yek."

He said, "I'd say Mrs. T.'s guess is closer.

"Would you believe I lost a bag of green grass hoppers back at Bird Street?

"I was right behind Mr. Lee when he was spying on you guys.

"Could I help it if all my bugs happened to escape onto his back?"

Kathy gasped, "Sammy, you're kidding! What if he had seen you? And those poor insects!"

Sammy said, "Those little guys WANTED to get out. It was a lot better than being used for bird food."

Bill said, "Come on, let's move along before Sammy gets us ALL buggy. Time to go to the Star Ferry and cross to the island."

At last they reached the ferry boat and boarded it.

The crew un-tied the ropes.

The huge, heavy boat floated slowly toward Hong Kong Island.

Sammy said, "I love this ferry! It's so cool riding like this. Hey, do we have to go to the street booths today?

"How about sticking with the ferry? Back and forth, back and forth. It'll drive Mr. Lee up a wall!"

So they rode the ferry all afternoon ... stopping only for a bowl of juicy noodles.

Sammy's face was a mess, and so was

the front of his shirt. He said, "Boy, good thing we learned how to use chopsticks in Japan! Now we are experts!"

Bill laughed, "Sure, Sammy! Expert mess-makers!"

The Woodlanders explored all they could for three days. They went ...

to the zoo

to the city gardens

on a wild bus ride into the mountains

to the open-air food markets

... and the whole time a man wearing dark glasses followed them.

Limp as old rags, the Woodlanders flopped into bed Friday night.

In ten minutes they were in a deep sleep. Then ...

BR-R-R-R-RING!

BR-R-R-R-RING!

BR-R-R-R-RING!

A fire alarm rang out in the middle of the night!

Loud and scary, it woke everyone in the hotel.

Dave pulled himself into his wheelchair.

The Woodlanders raced through the fire door with a crowd of other guests.

They lowered Dave's chair down the first two flights of cement steps. They could hear emergency trucks roaring up the street.

People in their pajamas crowded down the stairwell with them.

Fire fighters carrying axes and wearing smoke masks ran up the steps past them.

Finally Dave said, "Hey, I don't even smell any smoke."

Bill said, "I don't think anything's really burning."

Then a loudspeaker blared in Chinese and then in English, "This was a false alarm, everyone. Sorry you were all put to this trouble. It is safe to return to your rooms."

Back in their room, Mrs. Tandy said, "Look! Someone's dumped my purse out onto the bed!"

The monster book was gone.

Sammy yelled, "THAT RAT! I bet Mr. Lee planned this whole thing! He scared hundreds of people just to get us out of our room!"

Dave said, "He wanted the book right away. He must be getting ready to leave

Hong Kong. I've got to phone Mr. Mori and tell him what's happened."

But the next day, Saturday, they were in for an even bigger surprise.

Chapter 11:
Mr. Lee's Next Surprise

Dave phoned Yoshi Mori that night.

Mr. Mori agreed that Bo Lee must be planning to leave Hong Kong soon.

He told Dave, "You probably won't be

seeing any more of him. Just enjoy the rest of your trip. My team will stay on Lee's trail from this point on."

He thanked them for all their help.

The Woodlanders decided to spend the next day shopping at the street booths.

Kathy took a look up the first street of booths. She said, "Oh my gosh!"

The whole street was only about as wide as a school hallway.

People were selling all sorts of things ... purses ... silk cloth ... umbrellas ... toys ... knives ... beads.

Shoppers jammed the street, looking, talking, buying.

Sammy said, "Hey! Look at this! And that! And this!"

He began pushing in every direction.

Bill grabbed him. "Sammy, we won't be able to stay near each other here! It's ten o'clock now.

"Let's just all meet every half an hour, at the end of each block."

One by one the Woodlanders all squeezed down the street. Then they met and started up the next one.

By noon they were loaded with things they had bought.

Sammy groaned, "This stuff is heavy! And hot! And slippery!"

With that, all his bags slipped out of his hands.

Dave said, "Never mind, Sammy. Someone go buy some string. We can tie the bags together."

Then he hung the bags from his wheelchair handles.

Bill said, "Why don't we head up to the street called Hollywood? That cracks me up ... Hollywood ... here in Hong Kong."

So they went to Hollywood Road and into the first store.

Mrs. Tandy said, "Isn't it great not to have to worry about Mr. Lee anymore? Now we can really enjoy ourselves."

Kathy added, "I never saw so many small, pretty things crowded into one store. Like these pottery dragon-dogs ... they call these foo dogs."

Dave said, "Look at these little statues. Those are seven Chinese gods and goddesses. And those statues are of the wise Buddha."

Sammy said, "BOO-duh? Oh, yeah, there are pictures of him every where!"

Mrs. Tandy said, "Look at these beads. And that bracelet! And these little wooden animals! How will we ever decide what to buy?

"I want to look in some other stores, too."

They headed out the door. Suddenly Sammy whispered, "Hey, guys! Look!"

They stopped walking and looked where he pointed, to the end of the block.

Two men were building a crate around a huge wooden statue. It was a statue of a really fat, happy Chinese man.

Dave said, "It's a Buddha!"

One man was screwing more boards onto the crate.

And the other man, standing next to him, was Bo Lee!

99

Mr. Lee was pointing and giving orders.

For a couple of minutes they watched and listened.

They saw Mr. Lee use the screwdriver himself.

Then he happened to look up. His eyes fell on the Woodlanders.

He took a quick step back and almost fell off the curb.

Then he pulled himself together and smiled at them.

He walked over to them and said, "I can't believe my eyes. You are ... you are my little friends from the plane to Japan!

"Imagine seeing you again, after all this time."

Sammy said, "Hey! What do you mean? You've been—"

He felt Bill poke him in the ribs. "You've been ... buying a really big Buddha statue there ... and you helped get it packed ... and everything."

Mr. Lee said, "Oh, no ... no. You have it all wrong.

"This isn't my statue. I just happened to be walking by. I stopped to watch it being packed."

He smiled a very fake smile.

The Woodlanders could tell he was worried. Or angry.

Suddenly he surprised them by saying,

101

"Tomorrow, Sunday, I have the use of a friend's sailboat.

"How would you all like to go for a trip on the China Sea?"

Sammy blurted out, "But ... what about your book? Aren't you going to ask about your book? For your grand-child?"

This time EVERYone poked him, HARD.

Dave explained, "We had a book you must have left with us by mistake ... but it seems now we've lost it."

Mr. Lee gave a smooth smile and a little laugh.

He said, "I lost track of you at customs. So I bought another copy. Don't think any more about it. That book was no big deal to me."

Sammy was looking like he smelled something bad ... but Bill poked him again, so he kept his mouth shut.

But Kathy spoke up. "About going sailing ... we'd love to ... but we will have a friend with us tomorrow. Could we bring him?"

Everyone looked at her, their mouths open in surprise.

By now Sammy had been poked so much, even he kept quiet.

Mr. Lee said, "Plenty of room. Bring your friend along."

When he asked them where they were staying, Sammy looked like he would explode.

Mr. Lee told them when he'd pick them up, and they left.

Bill shook his head. "Well, we were supposed to act friendly. But I'm nervous about going out sailing with him."

Sammy said, "Kathy, who the heck were you talking about to Mr. Lee? WHAT friend will be with us?"

Kathy said, "Well, I'm not sure exactly. But if we call Mr. Mori, I know he will send SOMEONE to protect us."

Sammy looked at her proudly.

He said, "Wow, Kathy! Why didn't I think of that? Well, I know I WOULD have, if you guys hadn't poked my brains out today.

"Anyway, there's no reason to worry about going sailing with him.

"It could be fun!"

Bill still looked worried. "Then why do I keep thinking of the woman in the song?

"You know, the one who sailed away on a bright and sunny day ... on the back of a crocodile ... and NEVER GOT BACK ALIVE!"

Sammy said, "Don't be such a chicken! What could possibly go wrong?"

Chapter 12:
A Sinking Feeling

At 7:00 the next morning the Woodlanders sat in the hotel lobby.

With them was a man named Paul Ho.

He carried a big tote bag, and was dressed in jeans and a long-sleeved shirt.

No one would guess he was from Interpol.

He and Sammy were playing cat's cradle with a piece of string.

Sammy was singing the crocodile song, for about the twentieth time.

Bill said, "Sammy, cut that out! That isn't funny anymore."

Mr. Lee walked in through the hotel door.

Dave whispered, "Something IS wrong. He looks too happy."

Sammy said, "It's OK. After all, there are six of us, and only one of Mr. Lee."

But Dave was worried. He said, "Just the same, be on your toes, guys."

Mr. Lee called, "Come along, everyone. The limo is ready to go!"

He nodded hello to Paul.

The limo was waiting for them outside the front door.

Sammy said, "Wow! It's the biggest limo I've ever seen! And the fanciest!"

So when they got to the dock they were surprised. The sailboat wasn't all that fancy.

It was a run-down, sorry-looking boat.

Its wooden sides were banged up.

Its paint was peeling.

Its sails were torn.

Its ropes were ragged.

Mr. Lee said, "Climb aboard and sit down. I handle the boat myself."

The Woodlanders lifted Dave in his chair onto the deck.

Mr. Lee pointed to steps that led below deck to a cabin. He said, "There's a head down there, and a galley."

Sammy looked scared. He said, "What do you mean? Whose head?"

Dave laughed. He said, "He means there's a ship's bathroom. That's called a head. And a galley is a ship's kitchen."

Mr. Lee said, "I'll have us out of the harbor in no time.

"When you're hungry, bring up the big basket you'll find in the galley. It's lunch!"

Sammy poked Bill. He whispered, "Hear that? Maybe Mr. Lee isn't as bad as I thought. He brought lunch!"

Kathy looked around. She said, "Mr. Lee, where are the life jackets?"

Mr. Lee said, "They are in the seat below you. But you won't need them."

Just the same Kathy asked everyone to get up. She lifted the seat top and looked inside to be sure.

By noon they had sailed far, far out of sight of the mainland.

They ate a wonderful lunch ... sandwiches ... fruits they had never tasted before ... dry-roasted salty beans ... and sweet black bean cakes.

Then Bill said, "Mr. Lee, shouldn't we start for home now? It will take quite a while for us to sail back."

But Mr. Lee said, "We will sail out a bit more. We can use the motor to return. The day light will be with us another few hours."

By 4:00 Dave realized they hadn't seen another boat for hours.

He said, "We must have left the fishing lanes. We are out here all alone. And it's a dead calm now. There's no wind for sailing.

"You'd better start that motor."

Just as he said that, they saw a boat, way out in the sea.

Dave said, "Look at that boat! Where did that come from? It looks like a little hydro-foil. And it's coming FAST!"

The hydro-foil came shooting toward their boat.

The driver slowed it down and lined it up with their boat.

With one quick move Mr. Lee jumped into the hydro-foil.

He pushed away the sailboat.

He grinned. He said, "I'm leaving. The sailboat's all yours. Oh, by the way,

I wouldn't try to use those life jackets. They don't float. And another thing. This water is full of sharks."

By now he was so far away he was shouting. "Your motor's dead! And there's a little surprise for you below deck!"

Then the hydro-foil sped away.

Paul Ho jumped over to the motor and tried to start it. No luck.

111

He said, "Don't worry."

He took a small two-way radio out of his tote bag. He called Interpol.

Then he said, "I've got inflatable life jackets with me, but I sure hope we won't have to use them.

"Interpol should pick us up any minute now."

Dave said, "Maybe we can find enough wind to sail."

Paul shook his head. "I'd guess not. Mr. Lee had a pretty good idea of where we were. He knew there would be almost no wind in this part of the China Sea.

"We will just have to wait to be picked up."

Sammy said, "Well, I'm going down into the galley. I'll bring up the leftovers from lunch. I wait better with my stomach full."

He went down to the galley. The next minute they heard him yell, "BILL! HELP! THE BOAT'S SINKING!"

Chapter 13:
The Discovery

Bill and Kathy climbed down to the galley.

Sammy was standing in water up to his ankles.

Bill shouted up, "We've got to get this water out, fast!"

Dave shouted back, "Come back up on deck! Paul, let's get the pump going!"

Seconds later, Paul said, "Lee's ruined the pump, too."

Mrs. Tandy said, "Paul, what's that you're pouring over-board?"

Paul said, "I saw a fin. This stuff is supposed to chase sharks away."

Mrs. Tandy whispered to herself, "Taking on water ... dark soon ... other boats could hit us ... sharks around ... "

Then she shouted, "Wait a minute! Do you hear what I hear?"

It was a motor.

A big hydro-foil came speeding toward them.

The Woodlanders began shouting and waving.

Sammy climbed up on a seat and

started to jump and wave.

Bill grabbed him and pulled him back down.

Sammy yelled, "You want to be a big old party-pooper?"

Bill yelled back, "You want to be a big old shark dinner? Now stay DOWN!"

They cheered as the Interpol boat pulled slowly up to them ... and they climbed safely on board.

The next morning the Woodlanders and Paul Ho boarded a plane to Los Angeles, California.

Mrs. Tandy said, "My, I'll be glad to get home. We will all need a week to rest up from this vacation!"

Paul said, "But there's one last job for you. Yoshi Mori is holding Bo Lee and the Buddha statue in L.A.

"We need you to say if it's the same

Buddha you saw him with."

Sammy said, "Boy, is that rat Mr. Lee going to be surprised to see us alive!"

After a long flight, and not much sleep, the Woodlanders were tired.

They dragged into the L.A. customs room with Paul Ho.

Yoshi Mori, this time wearing a business suit, greeted them with a bow.

Inside they saw Bo Lee, sitting with a calm smile on his face.

When they came in, Mr. Lee jumped to his feet. He looked almost sick at the sight of them.

Sammy couldn't hold back for a second. He shouted, "You big rat! You tried to drown us!

"I'm glad I let those bugs run all over your back on Bird Street!

"I wish I'd bought TWO packages, not just one!"

Bill tried to calm Sammy down.

It was no use.

Sammy kept right on shouting. "Now you're going to jail for trying to drown us!

"And besides that, the police know you hid diamonds in this Buddha!

"And we saw you crate it up! This very same one!"

By then Mr. Lee was purple with rage, but he fought to stay calm.

He said softly, "You brat. Who says I

was trying to drown you? It was just a joke. My boat man will swear I returned to pick you up.

"But when we got back, you were all gone, and the boat was gone.

"I will tell the judge how rude you are. He will believe I was just trying to scare you.

"And when they search the Buddha? They won't find a thing."

Yoshi Mori called his team in. He said, "Take Bo Lee out of here. Let the customs people get to work."

Paul Ho took the Woodlanders to a restaurant for an hour.

When they came back, the Buddha was out of its crate.

The boards that had made up the crate were lying on the floor around it.

Yoshi Mori said, "Bad news. We've run the statue through every test.

"We even tipped this huge thing onto its back. We searched it from the bottom.

"We thought there might be holes DRILLED into it. We used X rays. We used sound waves. We found nothing.

"This Buddha is clean."

Mr. Mori went on. "We can charge Bo Lee with trying to drown you ... but it looks like all our work to find out how he smuggles diamonds was a waste."

Just then a police officer brought Mr. Lee back into the room.

Sammy said, "RATS! I'm sure you've got those diamonds!"

He kicked one of the heavy boards from the crate.

He kicked it so hard, he hurt his toe. He grabbed his foot with his hand and hopped around the room.

The board rattled across the floor.

Mr. Lee gave a nervous jerk. He looked sick again.

Dave had been watching him. Suddenly he said, "Bill, hand me that board."

He turned it in every direction. He looked over every inch of it.

Bo Lee's hands became tight fists. His face grew shiny with sweat.

At last Dave said, "Mr. Mori, look at this little dark circle in the wood in the end of this board.

"Forget the statue! The diamonds aren't in it. I think they're inside these packing boards. Check THEM!"

A customs worker took the board. In a few minutes he came back. He said, "You are right, young man.

"Someone's drilled a hole into each end of this board.

"There are diamonds inside each hole.

"The holes are sealed with wooden pegs sanded smooth.

"Other boards must be done the same way.

"We've cut open one end of this one. The diamonds are inside a paper tube ... it looks like a page from a book with monster pictures in it."

Dave said, "So THAT'S how he's been doing it! He matched up the addresses in the monster book with the right diamonds!"

Mr. Mori said, "We've got him at last! Write up the charges, and take him away."

Then he turned to the Woodlanders. He said, "I owe you. I hope you will be my guests someday in Japan.

"But soon you'll be on your way home. What can I do to thank you?"

Bill said, "Nothing, Mr. Mori. We were glad to help."

But Sammy said, "I know something you can do. My toe hurts from kicking that board. And I've always wanted to ride in one of those airport carts.

"Do you think ... "

A minute later Mr. Mori and Mrs.

Tandy were sitting in one cart. Sammy and Paul were sitting in another. Bill, Kathy, and Dave were in a third one.

With their bags piled around them, they rode like kings and queens to the plane.

Then Mr. Mori handed Bill a package. He told him not to open it until they were on the plane. Then he bowed to each of them.

They all bowed back.

Then suddenly Sammy hugged Mr. Mori.

He said, "I had such a good time working for Interpol, I hate to say good-bye."

But it was time to get on board.

On the plane they opened Mr. Mori's present.

It was a copy of the monster book for each of them.

Inside each book he had written,

Thank you for helping catch
the worst monster of all.
From your friend,
Yoshi Mori

The Woodlanders looked at each other and grinned.

Then they lay back in their seats and slept, holding their monster books ... dreaming of bugs ... and sailboats ... and diamonds.